KU-406-071

B48 081 425 8   MSC

British Library Cataloguing in Publication Data
A catalogue record for this book is available from the British Library.

ISBN 0 340 85417 0 Hardback
ISBN 0 340 85418 9 Paperback

Text and illustrations copyright © Deborah Inkpen 2002

The right of Deborah Inkpen to be identified as the author and illustrator
of this Work has been asserted by her in accordance with
the Copyright, Designs and Patents Act 1988.

10 9 8 7 6 5 4 3 2 1

First published 2002
by Hodder Children's Books
a division of Hodder Headline Limited
338 Euston Road London NW1 3BH

Printed in Hong Kong

HARRIET
AND THE LITTLE FAT FAIRY

DEBORAH INKPEN

Hodder
Children's
Books

A division of Hodder Headline Limited

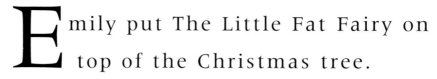

Emily put The Little Fat Fairy on
top of the Christmas tree.
'Now, don't fall off again!' she said.
The fairy smiled blankly.
Emily jumped down from the
chair and ran to Harriet's
cage. She lifted the
little hamster gently from
her nest.
'It's Christmas Eve,'
she whispered.

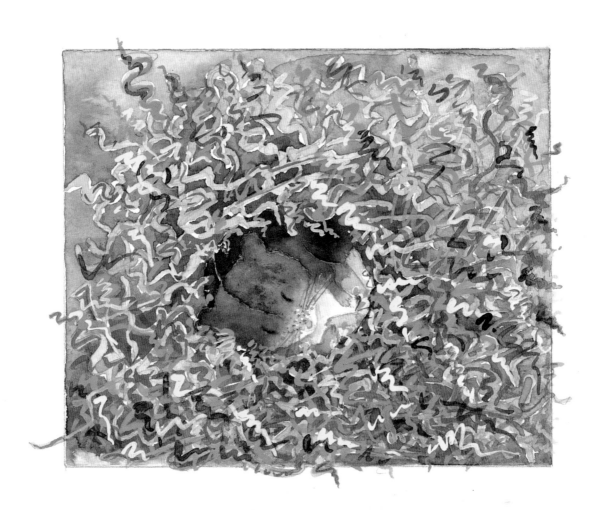

Emily took her over to the Christmas tree.

'Look,' she said stretching out her hand.

Harriet opened one eye. A huge, dark, spiky shape towered above her. It was covered in hundreds of fairy lights. They seemed to dance and twinkle all around her.

Harriet sniffed the air. It smelled of pine trees.

She crawled to the end of Emily's hand.
The pine needles prickled her nose.
She stretched a little further, lost her
balance and fell, landing upside down on one of
the branches.

Emily giggled. 'You don't make a
very good Christmas decoration,'
she said. She took some tinsel and
popped it on Harriet's head.

'That's better,' said Emily.

Harriet's tinsel floated to the floor. Emily caught it. When she looked up, Harriet had gone.

'Oh, no!' said Emily.

She peered into the branches. She could just make out Harriet's little pink nose. She dived under the tree, searching desperately through the maze of prickly branches and Christmas decorations.

Harriet had disappeared.

At the top of the tree The Little Fat Fairy continued to smile.

H arriet began to explore her sparkly,
new world. She peered into a shiny,
gold bauble. A funny little face peered back.

S he tried nibbling a red
plastic berry.
It was hard and tasteless.

Then she nibbled a
chocolate snowman.
That tasted better, once
she had chewed past the
silver paper.

Emily's brother Billy came to help.

They caught glimpses of Harriet, scampering through the branches but always just out of reach.

After a while they lost sight of her altogether. They sat down, their hands scratched and sore.

'She's probably left the tree by now,' said Billy. 'She could be anywhere!' Emily looked tearful.

'Let's put her cage under the Christmas tree,' he said. 'Perhaps she will find her own way home.'

Emily wrote a letter to Father Christmas. 'Dear Father Christmas, please can you bring back my hamster?'

Emily's mum warned her daughter, as she grabbed her hat and coat, that Father Christmas was very busy on Christmas Eve, and perhaps he would not have time to answer her letter.

Emily said she was sure he would. But her mother didn't hear. She had already left to go shopping.

Emily thought for a moment and then added,

'P.S. And could you bring her a friend?'

arriet had not left the Christmas tree.
She was busily climbing through the branches
and had come across some very curious things:

A tiny straw reindeer.

A tin Father Christmas.

A painted, cardboard
teddy bear,

and a little red basket,
which fitted her perfectly.

Emily and Billy spent the afternoon drawing until their mum returned from shopping. She was carrying a little white box with holes in the sides, which she took upstairs, before joining them for tea.

'Harriet's not back yet then?' she said. They shook their heads.

Emily had one last look under the tree before bedtime.

The cage was still empty.

'Don't worry,' said her mum, as she tucked
Emily into bed. 'I expect she will turn up.'
When she was sure that Emily and Billy were
fast asleep, Emily's mum picked up the box and
tiptoed downstairs to the Christmas tree. . .

At the top of the
Christmas tree Harriet
came face to face with The
Little Fat Fairy. As she
scrambled up on to the
fairy's shoulder, the slender
branch began to wobble.

They balanced there
for a moment, then the
fairy toppled forwards.
She tumbled down through
the branches, taking
Harriet with her.

H arriet landed with
a thud on top of
the fairy.

She rolled on to the floor. . .

. . .and sat up next to
her cage. Curled up inside
was a Russian hamster,
just like herself!

Harriet lay still for a moment, just watching, wondering what to do. She tried the cage door. It was shut tight. She ran up and down the bars. There was no way in.

The Little Fat Fairy lay near by. Exhausted from her adventure, Harriet nuzzled into the fairy's soft, shimmery jumper.

As she closed her eyes she heard the sound of sleigh bells. By the time Father Christmas arrived, Harriet was fast asleep.

When Emily came down on Christmas morning, Harriet was back in her cage, and she was not alone!

'Wow!' said Billy.

'Oh, my goodness!' said Mum. 'Three hamsters!'

'Father Christmas did answer my letter!' said Emily. 'I knew he would!'

As she bent down to open the cage, Emily spotted the fairy.

'Fallen off again?' she said. The Little Fat Fairy just smiled back.

To Adam,
S.McB.

For Di,
A.J.

First published 2007 by Walker Books Ltd
87 Vauxhall Walk, London SE11 5HJ

10 9 8 7 6 5 4 3 2 1

Text © 2007 Sam McBratney
Illustrations © 2007 Anita Jeram

Guess How Much I Love You™ is a registered
trademark of Walker Books Ltd, London

The right of Sam McBratney and Anita Jeram to be
identified as author and illustrator respectively of this
work has been asserted by them in accordance with
the Copyright, Designs and Patents Act 1988

This book has been typeset in Cochin

Printed and bound in China

British Library Cataloguing in
Publication Data: a catalogue record
for this book is available from the
British Library

ISBN 978-1-4063-0853-2

www.walkerbooks.co.uk

GUESS HOW MUCH I LOVE YOU

I LOVE YOU

in the

SPRING

Written by

Sam McBratney

Illustrated by

Anita Jeram

WALKER BOOKS
AND SUBSIDIARIES
LONDON · BOSTON · SYDNEY · AUCKLAND

Little Nutbrown Hare
and Big Nutbrown Hare went
hopping in the spring.

Spring is when things start
growing after winter.

They saw a tiny acorn growing.

"Someday it will be a tree,"
said Big Nutbrown Hare.

"A big big tree?"

"Oh, a mighty tree,"
said Big Nutbrown
Hare.

Little Nutbrown Hare spotted a tadpole
in a pool. It was a tiny tadpole,
as wriggly as
could be.

"It will grow up to be a frog,"
said Big Nutbrown Hare.

"Like that frog over there?"

"Just the same as that one,"
said Big Nutbrown Hare.

A hairy caterpillar slowly crossed the
path in front of them, in search of
something green to eat.

"One day soon it will change
into a butterfly," said
Big Nutbrown Hare.

"With wings?"

"Oh, lovely wings," said
Big Nutbrown Hare.

And then they found a bird's nest
among the rushes. It was full of eggs.

"What does an egg turn into?" asked
Little Nutbrown Hare.

"A bird."

"A big big bird?"

"Well ... a grown-up bird,"
said Big Nutbrown Hare.

Does nothing stay the same? thought Little Nutbrown Hare. Does everything change?

Then he began to laugh.

"What does a little
brown hare like
me turn into?"
he said.

Big Nutbrown Hare
began to think,

and think...

Goodness me, did he
know the answer?

Yes!

"A Big Nutbrown Hare – like me!"